Storming Jericho

More Erotic Romance

by Shelby Kent-Stewart

Surviving Sydney (Wicked Tails Series, Book 1)
Runaway Brat
Blessing (Wicked Tails Series, Book 2)
Once Upon a Faerie
Serenity's Child

Coming Soon

For Love of Honor (Wicked Tails Series, Book 3)

Storming Jericho

A novella by
Shelby Kent-Stewart

MORAN PRESS
LAS VEGAS, NEVADA

ISBN-13:   978-0997949117
ISBN-10:   0997949112

Chapter 1

"It's a simple question, Howard. Why is Rourke Simmons sending you a check for a thousand dollars and why does the memo say Jericho Kelly Trust? Since when do I have a trust?"

Seething on the inside, I nodded calmly at the check. I loved this man, I really did. Family friend and confidant, he'd been there for me through the worst days of my life, but if he tried to pacify me or lay some lawyer mumbo-jumbo on me, things would take a nosedive jiffy-quick.

"Have you done something different with your hair?"

"We were discussing the check, remember?" Not that the question surprised me. Since rolling out of bed, I'd done diddly but shower, slip on a pair of overalls and make a detour to the mailbox. My hair was a consequence of letting nature take its course and not giving a crap. I saw Simmons' name and panicked. After eight years of trying to forget that wretched night, it all came roaring back, every humiliating, excruciating second.

"You look pale, Coco. Would a cup of coffee would hit the spot?"

"Thanks but no. I don't want a cup of coffee and my name is Jericho. No one's called me that since Jeremy…" I still couldn't say the word aloud. It floated in the silence until I had to dip my head to clear the visions that crept in when I least wanted them. "You were Pop's best friend, Howard. I've always trusted you, so please be straight with me."

"I assume someone in his office made an error, a new employee, a secretary or assistant. She must have seen your name in the memo and addressed the envelope to you instead of me."

"Since when do cops have secretaries or assistants?"

Curiously, this was the first time since I'd stomped into his office unannounced that he looked surprised. "Rourke left the force within days of Jeremy's passing. I thought you knew."

Jeremy's passing. Why did people say that, as if he'd opened a door and gone from one room to the next. He'd died violently at the hands of monsters I'd see burn in hell if it was the last thing I did. "No, I didn't know. That explains the return address, RS something. I must have dropped the envelope by the mailbox."

"RS Investigations. Rourke got his P.I. license, and from what I understand, he has quite an operation going. At last count, he had a dozen agents working for him."

Rourke a private dick? How fitting. "Bully for him, but that still doesn't explain the check."

Despite my lousy track record with men, I knew surrender when I saw it and Howard may as well have been waving a white flag. "There's no easy way to tell you this, but since Jeremy's death, you've had a trio of, let's call them Guardian Angels." Correctly assuming I was ready to pitch a fit, he raised his hand. "And before you go off half-cocked, there are some things you should know. I loved your brother too, but his gambling problem was out of control. In a matter of six months, he went through the inheritance from your parents, including your college fund. When I saw the writing on the wall, I made him sign the family home over to you which, as you know, is free and clear thanks to your father's foresight. I don't doubt that Jeremy intended to try and recoup his losses but…"

"He died." There, I'd said it. The air around me stilled, the only sound the beating of my broken heart, but I'd deal with that later. At the moment, I was too appalled that Jace Malone, Blaine Thornton and Rourke 'shithead' Simmons had been providing the very food I ate. Who else could it be? "So for eight years his three best friends have taken it upon themselves to make me their charity case. They paid for my college education, my room and board, my clothes, everything?"

"They never saw you as a charity case, Jericho. You were eighteen years old with no family or available funds. You know as well as I those four men were as close as brothers. If the situation were reversed, I have every confidence Jeremy would have stepped up too."

It all made sense now, the chatty calls from Jace and Blaine while I was away at college. Since they were paying for it, they wanted to ensure they were getting their money's worth. On some rational level, I knew I should be grateful but being blindsided and having a nasty blast from the past was a lot to process for one morning.

That they could afford it was neither here nor there. Since leaving the force and taking his father-in-law's company public, Blaine was raking in millions; and Jace, dear Jace, half Sioux, half white, awesome and smart, the only one of Jeremy's three BFFs who could make me laugh when I was bawling my eyes out, now a successful author. They'd done well for themselves and I was happy for them, all but one and he could bite my butt.

"Please contact them today and remind them that I'm twenty-six, an adult not a child. I'm working so they needn't worry about me. I'll take care of this myself," I added, snatching back the check. "And one more thing. Let them know I intend to pay back every cent."

"They won't take a penny from you, but I'll relay your wishes. Are you sure about this? Free-lance writing assignments are iffy at best."

"I'm sure. As you pointed out, I'm living rent free and if I need to supplement my income until the writing gigs become more regular, I'll get a part-time job. I wish you'd told me but I understand why you didn't. Thanks for always being there." I took a deep breath and asked the question I always asked. Had I known the answer in advance, I would have saved it for another day. "I don't suppose there's been any progress on Jeremy's case."

Strange. I'd held this man's hand through the funerals of his wife of forty years, my brother and parents, and I don't think I'd ever seen him this defeated. "I was trying to find the right time to tell you. They've shut down the task force. There's no statute of limitations on murder and there's always a chance a witness will come forward, but it's only due to the pressure the boys put on the department that they kept it going this long. I'm sorry, sweetheart."

I'm not even sure I said good-bye. Stumbling from the office, I went in search of somewhere to regroup, someplace private where I could get my head on straight. I was peeling out of the parking lot when it hit me what I had to do. Whatever else my brother was, he was a good man, a good cop who deserved justice. No way would I let another eight years pass as his murder languished in a 'cold case' file. It wouldn't be the first time I'd ruffled feathers to get my way—and it wouldn't be the last.

Chapter 2

Jericho in trouble haul ass.

Jericho. The first time I ever saw her I remember thinking the name suited her just fine. With her fiery red pigtails and big green eyes, she pulled a pout, pink lips puffy and determined. I laughed and she glared back, a big expression for such a little snip. I knew right then and there that she'd be trouble. Big trouble. Damned if I wasn't right.

"Something funny you'd like to share, Rourke?" Snipping off the end of a cigar, Blaine Thornton hit me with the look I'd hoped to never see again. It was the same expression he wore the day he broke the news of Jeremy's murder with a lame cliché, the ending tacked on through a haze of whisky breath and smoke. *Only the good die young and we assholes are left to pick up the pieces.*

"I was thinking about the first time I saw her. It was Jeremy's twenty-first birthday and his folks threw him a party. She couldn't have been more than five or six but she had attitude to spare."

"Nothing much has changed. When was the last time you saw her?"

"The funeral." The day we buried my best friend and partner, the day I almost lost my mind and fucked his baby sister. Not my finest hour.

"That's bullshit, Rourke. You sat right here with Jace and me and promised…"

"I promised jack-shit. Like the two of you, I wanted to help out with her education and living expenses, whatever it took until she was firmly on her feet. I've kept my end of the deal, but I never promised to be her nursemaid or surrogate for her dead brother. Now why don't you get off your high-horse and explain why you sent me a cryptic five-word text and then turned off your fucking phone. Tell me why I drove all night, pissed in a paper cup instead of stopping and broke every speed limit between here and Austin."

"You tell me. For someone who claims not to care about her, you dropped everything to get here. I wonder why that is. You two have a history we don't know about?"

We had a history all right, one etched in stone that neither time nor distance could rewrite. A history that survived a career change, a bitter fiancée and a dozen other women who never measured up to the minx I kicked out of my bed one dark and stormy night. "Kiss my ass, Blaine. Start talking or I start walking."

In the chair next to mine, Jace tipped his Stetson over his eyes. "Wake me when you two lovebirds quit squabbling. If I wanted to hear pissing and moaning, I'd still be married to Alyssa."

"At least you got it right the second time around. How is Sabrina, that pretty little gal you were smart enough to marry?"

"Not happy with me right now. I left her with a scorched bottom and a butt plug. Should be an interesting homecoming."

"Asshole." Truth is, I owed Jace big-time. He was in the room next to mine that night, and there wasn't a chance in hell he didn't know what was going on, but he never breathed a word. "As much as I'd like to hear about your sex life, the only thing I want to do is grab that bottle of Jack and find a Motel 6, so either tell me what the brat did this time or…"

Folded into quarters, a newspaper landed on the coffee table between us, the words above the fold like a sharp knife to the gut:

**Sister of Murdered Cop Cites
Collusion Within Austin P.D.**

"Sonofabitch." I scanned the article but the rest was nothing but a rehash of bogus claims we'd heard before, how the department let down one of their own for not nailing the perps within the magical 48 hours. It was bullshit but the press ate it up. "We've waited all this time for the dust to settle and she pulls this. There's no way I can put a man undercover now, not with a spotlight on the case again. Do we know what prompted this stunt?"

"I can guess." Exhaling a puff of smoke, Blaine shook his head. "Howard called for an update last week. I was busy and forgot to return his call. I'm assuming he got itchy and called Ramirez. What's the Chief of Police going to do, lie? I'm sure Howard reported back to Jericho that the case was dead in the water, so she decided to make waves. I fucked up."

Yeah, he did, but I couldn't fault him for dropping the ball when I was never in the game. "I'll admit this is bad but maybe we're overreacting. We all know how these things play out. Tomorrow there will be another story. Let's give it a week or so and see how far the flak has flown."

"Better tell him, Hoss," said Jace, reaching for the bottle, a sure sign my day was about to go from bad to worse.

"Tell me what?"

"She's flying into Austin Friday to give a press conference and from there she's scheduled to appear on 'Good Morning Austin'. If I were a bettin' man, I'd say the flak is gonna hit the fan long before it flies. What do you think?"

I think instead of almost bedding her the night of Jeremy's funeral, I should have dragged her to the nearest Justice of the Peace, made an honest woman of her and provided the stability and guidance she never had from her socially-obsessed, globe-trotting parents or crazy-ass brother. Whatever else the years might have brought us, we damn sure wouldn't be having this discussion.

"You with us, Rourke?"

"Yeah, I'm with you." But I wasn't. The ache was back, the one that started in the pit of my stomach and worked its way to my balls every time I thought about her, which was way too often to keep a man sane. "Seems simple enough. Today's Tuesday. If one of you hops a plane for Connecticut tomorrow, you'll be there in time to talk some sense into her. Failing that, you can cuff her to a chair until Friday's come and gone. Once she's a no-show, the press will lose interest and that TV show won't be so all-fire eager to book her again."

"That just might work," said Blaine, his face a mask of brooding concentration. "Unfortunately, I have to be in London Thursday for a board meeting. What about you, Jace?"

"I wish I could but I'm on deadline. My editor's been chewing my ass for weeks."

Smiling for the first time since I arrived, Blaine pulled an airline ticket from his breast pocket and slapped it on the table. "Brilliant idea, Rourke. The guest room's all made up for you. Your flight to Hartford leaves midday tomorrow."

There's a saying that you never hear the bullet that takes you out, but I'd add one more thing to that. You never see it coming either.

Chapter 3

"I'm sorry, Maddie, but it's only for a couple of days. You know I have to do this, right? It's not like I'm running off to Fiji for an illicit tryst or anything."

There were times I suspected she read my mind, but even if she knew my thoughts went inevitably to Rourke, she wouldn't judge. Add to that the fact that she would never borrow my clothes and you have two of the many reasons my best friend is a dog.

As if I had any decent clothes to borrow. I'd been staring at my closet for half an hour and the only camera-appropriate *ensemble* I came up with was a wrinkled linen suit with 'bad karma' written all over it. I'd snagged it off a sale rack for an assignment I blew before I even made my pitch. Maybe sniping at the pissy receptionist wasn't the best way to endear myself, but I'm a Kelly after all. We punch first, ponder later. It's in our DNA.

Again my mind meandered to Rourke. Pissy fit him to a T, and for the millionth time I rejected Googling him. I'd had years to convince myself he wasn't the dashing hero I remembered, and what I thought was love was just a silly teenage crush. There wasn't a man alive who could match the God-like persona I'd created in my mind. Larger than life with his perfect face and body, he'd captured my heart from the time I was a little girl and waited until I was at my lowest to grind it into dust. To see the truth would only result in more drama, and my stress level was already off the charts, thank you very much.

I threw a few things in the suitcase and fought the rising panic of going public with my battle to keep my brother's case alive. Waiting for the axe to fall, I'd jumped at every ping on my computer, every jarring ringtone on my phone. I was sure Jace or Blaine would call, but as the clock ticked down it was plain they didn't care. My guardian angels had thrown in the towel, and with it any hope of their support.

The good news was I didn't have time to obsess about it further. I had an early morning flight and sufficient energy to take a long, hot bath, read a chapter of Jace's latest steamy thriller and grab a few hours of sleep before the airport shuttle came to pick me up.

That was the plan, but when my eyes popped open in the middle of the night, the odds favored I'd start the day on a gurney with a tag tied around my toe. Dark as a tomb, the room revealed nothing, and yet I felt a presence, a pro by all accounts. With a little know-how, an amateur might disable the alarm system, but only a professional could breach the defenses of a 130-pound Portuguese Water Dog in full-out protective mode.

Which clearly she was not. Snuggled next to me, she was snoring up a storm as my fingers crept beneath the pillow to snag my trusty .22. "You hurt my dog and I'll drop you where you stand. I have a gun."

With only seconds to discover the Walther MIA, I bolted upright as a disembodied chuckle rent the darkness followed by a voice I knew too well. "I wouldn't count on it. I'd have you on your back with your panties hanging from the bedpost before you fired off a round."

Fumbling for the bedside lamp, I closed my eyes against the light and opened them to find my worst nightmare lounging in my favorite reading chair. Tanned and buff with my .22 nestled against an impressive bulge, Rourke was every inch the Viking warrior I remembered—and then some. His hair was longer, the scruff along his jawline only upping his appeal, but it was the sexy grin that got me every time. Throwing back the blankets, I was up and in his face so fast it made my head spin. "You have thirty seconds to give me back my gun and leave or I start screaming bloody murder."

Those damn brown eyes met mine, and like a predator assessing prey, he looked me up and down, my body tingling in the wake. There was a time when I'd have given anything to have him gaze at me that way, but I was all grown up now and fairy tales were for little girls whose hearts were still intact. Reeling from his nearness, and despite my anger at his high-handed tactics, I blinked back tears. "Just go, Rourke. This is my battle and I don't want your help."

"I'm not here to help you make a fool of yourself."

"Since when? You had no problem helping me make a fool of myself eight years ago." I regretted those words before they even left my lips, not because they were untrue, but because now we both knew the truth, that part of me was still locked in some godforsaken place to which only he held the key.

"That's something else we need to talk about."

"We said everything we had to say the last time we were in this room." I've no doubt that line would have carried more weight had my boy-shorts not been drenched and my nipples poking through the gauzy top, but the horse was already out of the barn so what the hell. Let him look. I should have known the rat would turn the tables on me. The grin was gone and in its place was an expression I dare not put a name to. "You can save the smoldering glances for your groupies. I've moved on to men who want me, and I don't like sequels, especially when the ending sucks."

~~~

"You've changed, Red." Another lie, another flawed deception. It was a damn dumb thing to say but that crack about moving on purely pissed me off. On the outside, she hadn't changed a bit, same green eyes, same fiery red hair, a body to kill for, a face to die for. The last time I saw her, she was a girl inside a grown-up body, but this was a woman to be reckoned with, one who might not be so easy to leave.

"People change, Rourke, everyone but you. You're still the most cocky, most insufferable…"

"Insufferable? Is that one of those highfalutin' writer words?"

"Give me a break. Does that good ol' boy stuff really work on Texas girls? They must be disappointed when they discover you're a Connecticut Yankee, a Yale grad at that."

"You know, for someone who's moved on, you seem overly preoccupied with my sex life."

Bristling, she caught herself and feigned an indifference that was downright comical. "I couldn't care less about your sex life. I was just making conversation. You're the one who wanted to talk."

"You call this talking?"

"What do you call it?"

"Foreplay." I caught her wrists and penned her arms behind her. Drawing her close, I felt the pounding of her heart, the addictive scent of her arousal igniting every primal instinct plus a few I never knew I had.

She stiffened, her breath warm and sweet against my face. "Let me go."

"I don't think you've moved on at all. Say the words, Jericho, just the way you said them that night."

"Why, so you can reject me again?" Her eyes brimmed with tears, and I realized the damage I'd done; but she wasn't finished with me yet. The knife wasn't in nearly deep enough. "I was so scared, so alone. I thought if anyone could keep the monsters away it would be you. I wasn't looking for sex. I was looking for warmth, someone to hold me and tell me it would be okay."

"Baby, you'd just turned eighteen and I was thirty-two. I couldn't wrap my head around any of it, the age difference, my partner lying in a box while I'm lusting after his kid sister. I lost it when you said you loved me. I was in a dark place but I had sense enough to know there was no way I could be in the same bed with you without fucking you. I'll admit I could have handled it better. We looked everywhere for you the next morning before we left for the airport. I wanted to explain but all I found was a polite note thanking us for coming and saying you needed to get away for a few days. Where did you go anyway? I worried about you the whole damn flight."

"You were so worried that for almost a decade, instead of picking up the phone or sending me a lousy email, you soothed your conscience by writing checks. The joke's on you, Rourke. I never loved you. You were a convenient port in the storm. It could have just as easily been Jace." Wriggling free, her tone was cold, the distance she put between us measured not in feet but in wasted years of loneliness and grief. "The speech was great, by the way. It's your timing that's suspicious. I know you flew here to talk me out of it, but you came a long way for nothing. I'm more determined than ever to seek justice for my brother. You remember him, right, your best friend?"

"Are you finished?"

"With you, yes." A low rumbling from the bed caused us both to do a double-take at the pup still out like a light. "What did you do to Maddie?"

"A mild doggie-downer. She'll be fine."

"You're really something, you know that? You by-pass my alarm, drug my dog and sneak in here to watch me sleep like some psycho cat burglar." Green eyes blazing, she turned on her heel for the door, that gorgeous ass mocking me with every step she took. "I don't have time for this. I need coffee, a shower, and then I have a plane to catch. You know your way out."

"You're making a mistake." One of us was, and I was beginning to think it was me. I was crazy to think I could storm in here and rekindle feelings she never had when handcuffs and a ball-gag would have been a better plan. The longer I was with her, the more that crap about moving on stuck in my craw, not to mention the remark about Jace that stung like a sonofabitch. She had to have men crawling all over her. She was the worst kind of trouble, a woman who'd drive any man stark-raving mad—and make him grateful for the trip. Just when I was considering calling this whole fiasco a bust, she hurled a parting shot over her shoulder and it looked like I wouldn't be going anywhere, not today, maybe never.

"I've made a lot of mistakes but none ever cost me half as much as loving you."

Chapter 4

Dumb. Just. Dumb. Seeking sanctuary in the kitchen instead of locking myself in the bathroom, I realized my mistake too late. From the very instant he touched me, the ground gave way beneath me and I was falling harder than before, my libido short-circuiting my brain. But the dumbest thing by far was going off-script and negating every good intention I had to play it cool. *Say my peace, leave the room and zip it; but do not, repeat do not, ever try to have the last word with a man like Rourke 'The Rat' Simmons'.*

No sooner had I formed those thoughts when he strolled into the kitchen and proved me right. "You want to run that by me again?"

"Which part?"

"The part about loving me."

Flustered by his nearness, I'd have sooner taken a bullet than let him see me squirm, so I did what any self-respecting woman would do when she's caught with her proverbial panties down. I hit him with the *smile of death*. "You're hearing things, a condition not uncommon in men of your advanced age. It has something to do with an excess of arrogance. You might want to have that checked out."

He did have a nice laugh. For a rat.

Stepping up behind me, he swept my hair aside and brushed his lips against my neck. "I'd rather check you out. Put your hands on the countertop."

The husky timbre of his voice was the final irony, the voice I most wanted to hear, yet feared. The voice I'd conjured in my daydreams more times than I could count. Knowing I should run, the feel of his hard body at my back, his lips warm and firm against my skin, sent my hormones into hyper-drive, and like a fool I did as he asked. "Now what?"

"Now this," he whispered as he eased a hand beneath my top while the other inched inside my shorts. Rasping an eager nipple, he slid one long finger between my slick nether lips and took me to a place I'd only fantasized about. The pressure building, my breath came out in gasps, eight years of heartache dissolving in a hunger only he could sate.

"Please."

"Good girl."

Good girl. Two silly words and I imploded, all my nerve-endings set ablaze. So different from the brusque man I remembered, he held me as I spiraled out of control; and even through the aftershocks, he was there. It ended when my sanity returned and with it my resolve. What I failed to consider was his vast experience with women, his ability to read my body language and post-orgasmic paranoia for what it was: mind-numbing terror that when this was over, I'd be left in ruins.

"Look at me." Turning me to face him, he cupped my face, but where I expected to see a self-satisfied grin, I saw a man in turmoil. "You were right. I came here prepared to do whatever it took to keep you from that damn press conference and TV show. What I didn't count on was…"

Rarely at a loss for words, he surprised me with his hesitation, the way he stared at me. Hardly longer than a few seconds, it was time enough to plant a seed of hope. "Was what?"

"You. I didn't count on you." He took my lips in a frenzy of carnal need, and I matched it with my own. Drowning in sensation, I loved his taste, his touch, the way we fit together, an intoxicating fusion of the foreign and familiar. Long after it was over, he was still leaving a trail of tiny kisses on my eyes, my cheeks and even in my hair; and all the while a million questions rattled around inside my head, but the only one that mattered was the one I wouldn't ask. Would I ever occupy a small place in his heart? I laid my cheek against his chest and heard him draw a breath, but with his next words my own heart stopping beating altogether. "I should be lying in that box, not him."

I must have tensed and he drew back, but it never occurred to me to run. Perhaps it should have, but it didn't. Brushing a kiss across his cheek, I touched my fingers to his mouth. "Don't ever say that. I read the police report. It was a collar that went bad."

His eyes grew dark and hooded, the hesitation longer this time, and I feared the worst. I was debating if I could survive another round of unrequited love when he swept me up and carried me from the kitchen. "I need a shower."

It was so incongruous, so thoroughly unexpected that I laughed. "I have a plane to catch."

"There's a red-eye out tonight. If you still want to take it after I'm finished with you, I'll drive you to the airport."

"That's eighteen hours from now. What did you have in mind to do in the meantime?"

"Make up for eight years of being an asshole."

Chapter 5

She was still laughing when I dropped her on the bed. As much as I liked the sound of it, what I wanted to hear was my name on those puffy pink lips as she flew apart beneath me, my cock buried inside her to the hilt.

The laughter dwindled, and I saw the wheels turning as her eyes flicked here and there but never meeting mine. When we finally connected, we were locked in a skirmish neither wanted, her face veiled in sadness and distrust. A few minutes of alone-time seemed the wisest course. She needed space and I needed to take care of the hard-on I'd been fighting for an hour. There was no chance I could concentrate on her problem until I took my own in hand. "Your call, Princess. I'll grab a shower and then we'll talk."

"Wait."

Just seconds from a clean getaway, I was almost out the door when I turned to find her standing by the bed. Naked as a newborn, her skin flushed, that flaming mane all tossed and tousled, she bit her lip and it was one of those images that would stick with me forever; but it was when she squared her shoulders and walked toward me that I almost lost my shit. "Christ, you're beautiful." At the very least, I thought I'd draw a smile from her but this was no silly female placated by flattery. This was a woman hell-bent on staking her claim. My woman.

She stopped mere inches from me, so close I felt the heat rolling off her in waves. "I'm not a Princess and I'm not a good girl either. You asked me where I went the night I left. I drove for hours and ended up at Howard's lake house in New Hampshire. I knew where he kept the key and I helped myself to everything, including his liquor. I was there a week and when I wasn't drinking I was…"

"Go on."

"There was a bar down the road that catered to off-duty cops and firemen. Don't you see? I needed to know… "

"Stop." I'd known my share of rage but jealousy was new to me. It tore me up inside, and there was nothing gentle in the way I gripped her hair and forced her eyes to mine. "Do you have any idea what could have happened to you? I should take you over my knee and whip your ass."

She rolled her eyes, but judging by the way her cheeks tinged pink and her breath sped up, it was a safe bet that a good old-fashioned, bare-assed spanking had crossed her mind a time or two. "You sound like Jace or one of those macho characters from his books."

"You bet I do and I'm beginning to think he has the right idea. That wife of his is a handful too, but I've never seen two people more in love." I waited a beat before releasing her and adding the words long overdue. "Until now."

It's strange the things you remember about a person, quirks that define them and stay with you through the years. Small things mostly, a cock of the head, a look, a sigh. I'd watched her grow from tyke to holy terror and witnessed how she handled the worst days of her life, the way she wrapped her arms around her middle to protect herself. I'd seen her do it way too often, but it damn near killed me when she did it now. "That's not funny, Rourke."

"You see me laughing?"

"No one falls in love that fast, not even in romance novels."

"I wouldn't know about that, but there's a reason I left a perfectly nice woman standing at the altar in front of three hundred people. When I saw her walking down the aisle toward me, I knew I couldn't go through with it because she wasn't you."

The pull was strong, the need to put the past behind us like an itch I had to scratch. "I love you, Red. God knows, I've fought it, but there it is."

Eyes wide and wary, she laid her hands against my chest. It seemed an eternity before the corners of her mouth lifted in the sweetest smile I'd ever seen. "I've loved you all my life. Are you sure?"

"Come with me." I took her hand and all but yanked her from the room.

As I led her down the stairwell, she gave a last glance back toward the bedroom. "I can think of better ways to celebrate the occasion."

"There's something I need to do first."

"But I'm naked."

"Yeah, I noticed, so the sooner we get this over with the better." Rounding the corner to the kitchen, I hoisted her to the countertop and made a beeline for the fridge. She was already giggling a blue streak when I threw open the door, and I vowed that if I had to crawl through fire every day for the rest of my life, I'd keep her happy or die in the attempt.

~~~

I couldn't believe this was happening. If I awakened to find it all a dream, it would still be worth it. Watching him rummage through my refrigerator was the most fun I'd had in years. "Sorry, sailor. If you're looking for the whipped cream, I'm fresh out."

"You're a kinky little thing."

"Said the guy holding a bag of cucumbers."

When he turned around, the plastic bag was gone and he was fiddling with the little metal bag tie. "Unless you want me to make good on that spanking, you'll let me finish before you start arguing." He took my left hand and slipped something on my finger, a ring he'd fashioned from that silly metal tie. "This is temporary until I can replace it. After what happened to Jeremy, I kept my distance out of guilt but that doesn't mean I haven't loved you every goddamn day. I know it's sudden, but I don't want to spend another night without you in my bed. I want to reach for you and watch those gorgeous eyes soften in passion as I take you nice and slow. I want to hear you giggle and make you smile. I want yours to be the first scent I smell when I wake up, and your face to be the last thing I see before I fall asleep."

He needn't have worried about me interrupting him. I couldn't think of anything to say, another first.

"Well?"

"Was there a question in there?"

"Marry me?"

Kicking cool, calm and collected to the curb, I launched myself into his arms. "Yes. Yes!"

He caught me easily, and with my legs wrapped around him and his large hands cupping my bottom, his laughter echoed off the walls. "You sure you don't want to think about it?"

"Do you want me to?"

"Too late now, but there's something else we need to talk about. I bought a ranch, a few hundred acres outside of Austin. I know you love to ride but I also know your life is here, so I was thinking…"

"My life is wherever you are. It always has been, but please don't break my heart."

"I'd eat my gun before I let that happen." There was that look again, the one that made me melt, the one I knew deep in my soul that he reserved for me. "I don't know how I stayed away from you this long."

Floating weightless in his hands, I tugged the t-shirt up and over his head, the perfection of his body sending tremors to my core. I was so utterly happy and caught up in the moment that I barely noticed when he carried me to the stairwell; but with each step my ardor gave way to angst. Despite coming clean about hell-week in New Hampshire, there was one small detail I omitted. I recalled almost nothing of the hook-ups except I wanted them to end. Sadder still, the intervening years had done little to improve my technique, the few men I'd invited to my bed failing to light a spark, much less a fire. What if it was me? What if after waiting all these years, I couldn't meet his needs?

"Sweetheart, you with me here?"

Over-thinking things as usual, I almost missed the part where he set me on my feet and doffed his jeans and boxers. "Oh, my."

"I'll take that as a yes." When I finally pulled my eyes from the daunting erection bobbing between us, he had the water running in the shower and a finger curled beneath my chin. "You nervous, Red?"

"Petrified. About those other men…"

"What men?"

I could tell by his grin that he was teasing me, but it was exactly what I needed. I knew then why I'd sought release in the arms of other men and found only regret. This is where I belonged, where I was meant to be. Encouraged by his smile, I followed him into the shower, the water raising goosebumps on my overheated flesh. Of all my fantasies, this one always got me off. I'd close my eyes and imagine it was his hands soaping my body, no spot too intimate or off-limits; but this time when I opened mine, he was there, his own eyes black with lust.

It started with a nip, a lick, tongues dancing, whispered words and whimpers. Like a man possessed and I his willing demon, he stroked and fondled me into a delirium beyond my wildest dreams. When he lifted me and impaled me on his cock, I was wet and ready, each thrust a testament to his control, his power over me.

Lost in a fog of desire, I have no idea how long we lingered there pleasuring each other. Minutes? Hours? And when at last he toweled me dry and carried me to bed, I glanced at that lovely metal tie and smiled at the memory of the last few hours and how very different my life was now. With the promise of a future and a soft kiss on my lips, I fell instantly asleep.

Chapter 6

Notwithstanding that the only shut-eye I'd had in thirty-six hours was a brief nap on the plane, sleep was the last thing on my mind. I'd tasted her sweet essence and fucked her breathless but I needed more. I wanted to imprint the feel of her body entangled with mine and memorize each detail of her face. When I finally drifted off, it was into a world where beauty didn't exist, only violence and blood and the image of Jeremy, his bullet-riddled corpse on a slab.

"Rourke, honey, wake up. Please come back to me."

It was her soft voice and hand against my cheek that brought me back. It was awhile since I'd had a nightmare that bad, and I'd been known to thrash around, even break a lamp and knock a picture off the wall. That I might have hurt her made my blood run cold. "I'm sorry, Red. If I lashed out at you…"

"Shh, I'm fine. You were mumbling about someone named MacGyver. Who is he? Unless you'd rather not talk about it."

"It was a TV show in the late eighties, early nineties. You were just a baby when it aired. MacGyver was the character's name, some kind of secret agent. He didn't carry a gun but he could make a thermonuclear device out of a box of Cheerios." There was more to it, a lot more, but now was not the time and definitely not the place. Just lying there next to her with her face flushed from sleep, eyes damp and dewy, I was hard as a rock. Letting my arms take my weight, I rolled on top of her and kissed her nose. "I'd rather talk about us."

Her smile caused a slow burn to my balls as she reached between us and placed her hand around my cock. "You call this talking?"

"What do you call it?"

"Foreplay." She pushed against me, pinned me down and straddled me, lowering her body a little at a time until she took every grateful inch.

Finding heaven in her tight, wet warmth, I rose to a sitting position. She looped her legs around my hips, and as her eyes fluttered close, she bowed her back, her breasts an offering I couldn't refuse. I latched on to one nipple and then the other, worshiping them with my lips and tongue and teeth until I felt her climax building. Her channel quivering around me, she came screaming my name and I was dead certain if I died right then, I'd die a happy man. I was right behind her and we collapsed in each other's arms, the silence broken only by our mingled breaths and moans.

A quick nap, another shower and the best Huevos Rancheros I'd ever had and we were back in bed. Only this time I was determined to get a few things off my chest, including full-disclosure of the reason I was here and the ruse that got me on that plane. She never came out and said it, but I had the uneasy feeling she thought I volunteered which, despite the way things turned out, couldn't be further from the truth.

It might have been the way she whipped up brunch wearing nothing but an apron tied around her waist, her sense of humor, her easy laughter, the way her face lit up when I tugged her away from the stove to steal a kiss and cop a feel, how she trusted me after all the shit I'd put her through, but I was determined not to fuck up what we had by starting our life together with a lie. I also knew Jericho, and if I didn't handle it right and ease into the subject, it would be my balls hanging from the bedpost long before her panties.

~~~

"So what's with the elaborate security system?"

Either I was mellowing or simply sex-saturated, but instead of peppering him with questions, I was content to cuddle next to him. The details of the nightmare could wait. It bothered him, I knew it did, but I was more than happy to let him distract me with small talk. For now. "I had a couple of break-ins, the first a few weeks after Jeremy's funeral, the second six months later. I was away at school both times."

"What did they take?"

"That's the weird part. The security company called me when the alarm went off and I rushed home, but I couldn't find anything missing. Even my mother's jewelry was accounted for. The police came the first time, took a statement and said it was probably a malfunction in the system. I didn't call them the second time. What was the point?"

"But you don't believe it was a malfunction."

"I know someone was in the house. I could feel it."

"Did you tell Jace or Blaine?"

"It never occurred to me to tell them. What could they do, except suggest I upgrade my security, which I did the day after the second break-in."

"Is that when you bought the gun?"

"It was Jeremy's. I found it when I was going through his things." I didn't mention there were things I never had the courage to deal with, including a book he'd sent me the day he died, a signed copy of 'Angels and Demons' by Dan Brown. It was in the bookcase across the room and tucked inside was a sealed letter with my name scrawled on the envelope and instructions to read it in the event of his death. Whether due to cowardice or the fact that I'd only recently come to terms with his murder, I never opened it. Sooner or later I'd have to read it. But not today.

"I'm sorry, Red. I should have been here to help you with that. I should have been here for a lot of things."

"Ancient history. There's more to the MacGyver story than you told me, isn't there?"

A cloud passed over his features, a sign I'd steered us into choppy waters, but before I could retract the question, he took a breath and set his jaw. "We'd been planning that bust for weeks. Even the weather was cooperating. I was point-man. Jace and Blaine would be in the van monitoring the operation and coordinating reinforcements if we needed them."

"Where was Jeremy?"

"He was my back-up, at least that was the plan. When he didn't make the morning meeting, Blaine went to his apartment but Jeremy was still in bed and in bad shape from partying the night before. They had words and Blaine told him he needed to clean up his act. It escalated from there and Blaine finally kicked him off the operation. Jeremy asked him who the hell he thought he was, fucking MacGyver? Up till then, it was a joke among us but that day everything changed."

"He kicked him off the operation? I don't understand. Then how…"

When my voice faltered, he pressed a kiss to my forehead. "It was a cluster-fuck from the beginning. Blaine had just left Jeremy's apartment when Jace and I got a call from the D.A.'s office advising they needed us back in court. We'd both been testifying in a murder case for a week and we thought we were finished. As it turned out, we were. There was a screw-up in the prosecutor's office. By the time we got to court and found out the defendant had copped a plea, it was all over and Jeremy was dead. Blaine was in the process of cancelling the operation when he heard gun fire and Jeremy was down. He never had a chance."

"And you blame yourself?"

"Don't you?"

"No, I don't. You remember how it was when our parents died. He was everything to me, but I had no illusions about him even then. Since his death, I've tried to make him into some kind of saint, but he wasn't. I suppose at the end he wanted to redeem himself. In my eyes, he'll always be a hero but he was also a hothead."

"Says the woman who wanted to shoot my dick off."

His grin reassured me the storm had passed, and I snuggled closer. "I may be a hothead but I'm not stupid. I'm confused by something, though. A month ago, Howard told me one of the men arrested after Jeremy's murder was ready to give up the head honcho in exchange for a deal. If that's true and they were close, why did Ramirez disband the task force?"

"I asked Ramirez to shut it down. Before the guy could finger his boss, he was found dead in his cell with a knife in his back, and the task force was back to square one. If we had a chance of finding the ringleader responsible for Jeremy's murder, we had to come at it from another angle."

"We?" And then I got it. The investigation was going forward, only this time Rourke was at the helm. "RS Investigations. Your people could work with less restrictions and more latitude. I ruined everything with the newspaper article, didn't I?"

"You had no way of knowing, but when it comes to an undercover op, any news is bad news. Monsters like the one responsible for taking Jeremy out crawl back in their holes when you shine a light on them."

Lulled by his voice and concentrating on the big picture, I'd missed the details, but the more I thought about it, something didn't jibe with what I knew. Slipping from the bed, I found what I was looking for in the bottom drawer of my writing desk where

I'd stashed it eight years ago. The padded packaging was still intact, the postmark clear.

"Red, are you okay?"

My mind racing a mile a minute, I handed off the envelope. "Jeremy was pronounced dead at 10:33 a.m. on January 27th, 2007. Look at the postmark, Rourke. If he was still in bed hungover and if things went down the way Blaine said they did, he must have mailed it when he left his apartment on the way to the bust."

"That's a lot of 'ifs'. What are you getting at?"

"I'm not sure but something doesn't feel right."

In full cop-mode, he examined the envelope front and back, even reaching inside. "What was in here?"

"A book." I don't know why I didn't comment on the letter or why I felt compelled to grab my robe and slip it on. It might have been Maddie's whining at the door of the guest room where Rourke had carried her to sleep it off; but I know in my heart it was instinct, a premonition coupled with an overwhelming sense of doom, the chilling revelation that everything I thought I knew about love and loyalty were myths, another chapter in the same old tired fairy tale.

As it happens, I was right.

Chapter 7

"This is cozy."

My attention divided between the envelope and Jericho, it took a second to register the figure in the doorway. "Are you lost? I thought you had a Board Meeting in London."

Any worry I had that Blaine's untimely intrusion would freak her out was dispelled when Jericho lanced him with a glare and enough acid in her tone to melt a railroad spike. "Another Board Meeting? That's odd. You emailed me from London two weeks ago and wrote you fell asleep in the middle of it, don't you remember?"

"What's going on, Blaine?"

"I was about to ask you the same thing, friend. The plan was to keep her occupied, not fuck her. If I'd known that was the strategy, I'd have come myself." With a lingering leer that got my blood up, he gave a nod in my direction. "Did he tell you how ticked-off he was when Jace and I tricked him into coming here?"

Her eyes bore into mine with no emotion whatsoever, just ice. "He told me everything."

"Things have changed, baby."

"You're right, they have." Blaine's movements were a blur. Before I could pull my gun from beneath the blanket, he was pointing his at Jericho. "Don't even think about it or I'll blow her head off. This will go down my way, a murder-suicide of two ill-fated lovers. Thanks to that article of hers, it was the perfect opportunity to solve two problems for the price of a plane ticket. Now, put the gun on the floor and slide it over here with your foot. I'd hate to see her brains splattered all over this pretty wallpaper."

"Shoot him, Rourke. He won't kill me. I have something he wants."

"I always knew you had the brains in the family. The gun, old buddy. Now."

I'd have liked nothing better than to take the asshole out, but with his gun levelled at her head, I wasn't taking any chances. Hostage situations were tricky at best. When they involved someone you loved, the future mother of your children, they were hell on earth. Slowly, so as not to spook him, I followed his instructions to the letter.

"The package, Coco. Where is it?"

Her composure rock-solid, she huffed out a laugh. "Screw you, Blaine. You'll kill us anyway. You get the package when I get the truth. It was you who broke in here, wasn't it?"

Blaine's agitation was a red flag, a twitchy finger in close quarters topping the list of worst-case scenarios. The only hope I had of buying time was to keep talking. "One thing I always admired about Jeremy. Even when he was at his worst, he was a stickler for details. According to the sticker on this envelope, he sent it certified, which means he had a receipt on him when he died, something only the person in charge of collecting the evidence would know."

Damned if she didn't pick up the ball and run with it. "Someone close to the victim, who would never be questioned, a friend. The same person who could arrange a hit on a murderer trying to cut a deal."

"The same person who arranged that little fuck-up at the courthouse. While Jace and I were off chasing our tails, you sent Jeremy into that alley."

"My brother trusted you, you bastard. Why him, why us, why now?"

"Your brother had a big mouth, especially when he was hammered. We were at his apartment the night before the bust. He started talking shit, saying he'd been working on a theory. Let's just say it was a little too close for comfort. Why you? That should be obvious. You'll never let his death go and that's a risk I can't take. As far as your fuck buddy here, there's no way I can control his investigation, and things I can't control, I eliminate. You two make quite a team. It's a shame you'll never leave this room alive."

"Who are you working for, Blaine? What's the going price for my brother's life, for the lives of people you've known forever?"

"He's not working for anyone, honey. He's working for himself, aren't you, *old buddy*? You'd been grousing about wanting to leave the force for years, but you wanted to do it in style. When you took over your father-in-law's company, you were already a player."

"Yeah, so what? I wasn't born with a silver spoon shoved up my ass. I didn't go to Yale like you and Jeremy. I had to fight for every dime. I saw an opportunity and took it. I made a shitload of money selling drugs to losers. Give me the fucking package, Coco."

"You're too late. Your scheme backfired. For eight years I avoided opening the envelope because I didn't want to make his death real, and then Rourke showed up. We read it together and emailed a copy to Ramirez and the D.A.'s office. You're finished, Blaine."

"I think you're lying, but let's assume you aren't. I've racked up quite a body count already. What's two more? They can only stick the needle in my arm once. I'm not asking you again, Jericho. In thirty seconds, I start shooting and it's your choice whether it's the mutt or loverboy here."

"My vote goes to lover boy, but then I've always had a soft spot for Maddie. Drop it, Hoss, or it'll be your brains on the wallpaper, which would make me happy as a pig in shit."

Blaine's gun landed on the floor, and while Jace cuffed him, I grabbed my jeans off the floor. "You get all that?"

"Loud and clear, me and a carload of Feds who should be coming through the front door any minute to collect the trash." He paused and grinned at Jericho. "You did good, honey, but now you're not looking so red-hot. I'll turn this asshole over to the Ray-Ban brigade and the three of us will talk."

Pale and shaking from the adrenaline surge, she gripped the desk. "That's not necessary. I get the picture. It was all a scam."

"Not all of it, Red. That phone call earlier? It was Jace. After our meeting with Blaine on Tuesday, something didn't sit right with us either. He was too eager to get me here. We talked about it when Jace drove me to the airport and he decided to do some nosing around in Blaine's bank records. He went back ten years and hit pay dirt. There was no way of knowing he'd show up here, but we had a hunch he might. I didn't tell you because, from the very moment you turned on that light, I knew I had one shot with you to get it right this time."

I took a step toward her and she backed away. "Don't, Rourke. Just don't. Can I go now, Jace? I know I'll have to give a statement, but I really need to get out of here."

Turns out, looking down the barrel of the dirt-bag's gun was the easy part. The mop-up was the killer. "I realize this looks bad, but you can't throw away everything we had and run off again."

"Everything we had? We had twelve hours of lies interspersed with sex."

"Honey, hear the man out. I don't know what went down here but I know Rourke."

"Like you knew Blaine?" She pulled a book from a shelf and handed it to Jace. "There's a letter inside, which should put the nail in his coffin. I'm taking Maddie and leaving now, so unless you brought another pair of cuffs, get out of my way." Breezing between Jace and me, she got as far as the door before she stopped, picked up my gun, and held it out to me, grip-first. "Bon appétit."

Watching her traverse the dark suits approaching down the hallway, I was primed to go after her when Jace gave a low whistle. "That can't be good."

"It's not."

"You want some advice?"

"If it involves eating my gun, I'll pass."

"Let her cool down for a couple of days. Any idea where she's going?"

"Yep." I knew exactly where she'd run to, but if she thought she could replace me in her bed this time, she had a rude awakening coming.

"I've got one home just like her, so take it from me, no woman gets that riled unless she's in love. You two have been avoiding this showdown for years. If she were my woman, I'd track her down, tie her to the bed until she comes to her senses and get a ring on her finger. Think you can handle that?"

"Oh, yeah."

Chapter 8

With my knees hugged to my chest, I turned my face into the sun and let the tears dry on my cheeks. It was so much harder this time. The days were longer, the nights a never-ending cycle of anger and regret.

Eight years ago, I came here lost and found a semblance of myself. Not the perfect person I aspired to be, but a version of me. When I went back to face the world alone, I was wiser, stronger, harder. Or so I thought.

It was winter then, the snow knee-deep, the ancient pines like ghostly sentinels, ever watchful, always there. The lake was frozen over but still a melee of activity. A make-shift hockey rink dominated one end, the rest a playground for snowmobiles, their incessant rumble a cacophony of comfort.

Silence was the enemy, those hours between dusk and daybreak when I couldn't bear to be alone, when the demons came a-calling and I let them in. When in darkness I pretended it was Rourke's body entwined with mine, his lips and hands. His cock.

It's summer now and many things have changed, and yet remain the same. Instead of snow, pine needles carpet the ground. Snowmobiles are in storage and speedboats rule the day. And everywhere the sounds of joy and laughter. Everywhere but here.

Stretched out beside me on the dock with her chin resting on her paws, Maddie rolled her eyes in my direction and sighed. Her timing was so perfect that I almost laughed out loud. "I know, girl. Debbie Downer, right? He's a louse. We're better off without him."

Or were we? After three days of wallowing in self-pity, I wasn't sure. The nightmare with Blaine had rocked me and sent my emotions careening to the dark side. Was it possible I misread the situation and made Rourke another victim of Blaine's betrayal?

Mirroring my thoughts, a cloud eclipsed the sun—and then I heard the voice. "On your feet, Red, unless you want me to embarrass you in front of all these happy campers."

With water on three sides and a mountain of Alpha male on the other, I had no choice but to rise and stand my ground. "What do you want?"

"Nice outfit. What'd you do, mug a homeless person?"

"Not that it's any of your business, but I left in a hurry and only had time to grab a couple pairs of jeans and t-shirts. In case you haven't notice, it's freaking hot here. I may have gotten carried away with the scissors when I made the cut-offs and tank top but…wait a minute. I don't owe you an explanation for anything."

"If there were two more inches of fabric on those shorts, they might qualify as a thong."

"So now you're an authority on fashion? I don't know what you're doing here, but whatever you're selling this time, I'm not buying." Not much anyway. Even when he was scowling at me, he was delicious. Muscles rippling beneath the t-shirt and his man-scent like a drug, he set the standard for sexy.

I glanced away for half a second to get my bearings and he made his move. "Have it your way."

As I went flying over his shoulder, his hand connected with my ass and shocked the crap out of me. "Ouch, that hurt! You put me down, Rourke Simmons. I have nothing to say to you."

"Good. Let's keep it that way, because I have a lot to say to you."

Trudging up the hill with Maddie by our side, I made a few more failed attempts to wiggle from his grip, all of which earned me another stinging slap. By the time we reached the house, my butt was burning and I was so aroused I might have jumped him on the spot had I not spied his duffel bag in a corner of the bedroom and at least two dozen roses in a vase next to the bed; but as luck would have it, those weren't the only surprises. With the sheer drapes billowing in the breeze and two pair of velvet cuffs affixed to the antique four-poster, it was a scene out of every erotic novel I'd ever read. "What is this?" I asked, wobbling as he put me on my feet.

"What does it look like?"

"Jane Austen meets the Marquis de Sade."

"Close enough. Clothes off and hop up on the bed."

"I will not. You can't keep barging into my life and think…" But apparently he could. Before I could mouth a protest, I was flat on my back, my wrists bound in the cuffs. Despite my brain's best efforts to remain unaffected, my body disagreed as every cell coalesced into a single throbbing glob of hormones. "You do know I could have you arrested for breaking and entering, right? This is private property and it's not even my property. Okay, maybe I got permission this time, but that doesn't mean you can invade my privacy, leave your things and cuff me to a bed. Not that I don't appreciate the flowers but I'm still mad at you, so don't think because I did it once, I'll fall into your arms like some sex-crazed groupie."

"Woman, do you ever wind down? And who are all these groupies you keep referring to?"

"Seriously? Look at you, you're perfect. What woman wouldn't want you?"

"The one who drove two hundred miles to get away from me."

Struggling with the cuffs, I matched him glare for glare. "I was angry. You lied to me."

"That wasn't anger. It was a temper tantrum, and I never lied to you." Narrowed to slits, his eyes travelled slowly down my body, the telltale bulge in his jeans the icing on the cake. "Where are those scissors?"

"Why?"

"Because from now on, we're doing things my way. And while we're on the subject, there will be no more temper tantrums or running away when the going gets rough. I should have whipped your ass eight years ago and made an honest woman of you."

"Whipped my ass?" Had any other man threatened me or used that tone, I would have excised his scrotum with a serrated spoon, but every word he uttered caused another flutter in my tummy, another surge of moisture at the apex of my thighs. I could deny it, even fight it, but this was the man I wanted, the man I needed. Still, I wasn't ready to forfeit the game. Not quite yet. "If you think I'd ever consent to that 'head of household' nonsense, you're nuts."

"We'll see. Scissors. Now."

On the other hand, knowing when you're beaten has its perks. "On the dresser."

"Attached to this, are we?" He asked, turning from the dresser, the scissors in one hand, the metal tie between his fingers of the other.

"Maybe a little."

"Now that's a shame," he said and dropped it in the wastebasket.

"What are you doing?"

"Fulfilling a promise." And with that, he pulled something from his pocket and held it out for me to see. It was another ring, similar in shape and size to the other one but different, shinier. "I would have had it made in platinum but I know you like gold."

"You had that made for me? How, when? It's only been three days."

"You want something badly enough, you find a way."

"Are you going to release me so I can try it on?"

"Not on your life. I have you where I want you and, anyway, I'm saving it for the wedding. This time I'm not taking any chances. I figure if you're tempted to run from me again, the ring is a powerful inducement to stay."

As my eyes filled, I turned my face away. "You still want to marry me?"

With a tenderness that continued to amaze me, he cupped my cheek and brought it back around to meet him eye-to-eye. "More than ever, Red, but don't ever hide your tears from me again."

"My parents hated when I cried. They said well-bred young ladies never show emotion. I guess I have some issues to work through."

"We'll work through them together. The good times are even better when you share the bad."

Of all the things he might have said to me, none would have touched me more than that. "Are you real?"

He responded with a grin and sat beside me on the bed. I shivered when I felt the cold steel of the scissors but it was quick, and in no time at all the tank- top was in tatters, my breasts bared to his gaze. The shorts were next. Instead of cutting them, he pulled them off inch by inch, an exercise in frustration, to say the least. "Fucking beautiful."

"Then why are you still dressed?"

By way of a reply, he restrained my ankles in the other set of cuffs. Spread-eagled and at his mercy, I watched him pull a blindfold from his duffel bag and study me with yet another expression I'd never seen. Darker, more controlled, it was the look of a man who took what he wanted, and what he wanted most was me. "My show, my rules." Was the only thing he said as he tied the blindfold on.

It was the oddest sensation, as if floating on a cloud, no up, no down, no right, no wrong; but after several minutes without a sound, something stirred within me, a fear of the unknown.

Then I heard him whisper in my ear, "Relax, baby, and just go with it. I'll take care of you."

I whimpered as he nipped my lower lip, his touch like tiny lightning strikes against my skin. With a precision that brought me to the edge, he found my secret spots and made them his, my neck and wrists, behind my knees, all but one, the place between my legs that ached for only him. "Please."

"That's my girl." The blindfold came off first, followed by the ankle cuffs, and with my legs positioned over his shoulders, he took me in a single thrust and filled the void. Stroke after stroke, he claimed me as his own; and as we came together in that final moment of passion, I believed my world could not get any sweeter.

But I was wrong about that too.

With Jace and Sabrina in attendance, we were married a week later at our ranch. That was six months ago and it's amazing what I've learned. I learned that sometimes bad things happen to good people, but if we hold them in our hearts, they're always there.

I learned that any man can want you for your smile, but the one who wipes your tears and holds you through your pain is the one to whom you give your soul.

I learned that fairy tales are over-rated. Who wants to live in a boring castle anyway? I'll take the thrill of an amusement park where each new dawn brings something magical and exciting. Some days are up and down like a Ferris wheel or slow and easy like a Merry-Go-Round, but mostly they're a roller-coaster ride, a thrill-a-minute freefall that takes my breath away.

The secret is to buckle up, hang on tight—and keep the scissors handy.

About the Author

Born and raised in sunny Southern California, Shelby Kent-Stewart dissed the beach scene at an early age, preferring to while away the hours scribbling stories in her room. Very little has changed. She's still the geeky gal who rarely tans, drinks too much coffee and believes that making love—not war—will save us all.

She penned her first short story at ten, a woeful little tale about a girl searching for her boyfriend in Calais, France. To this day, She has no clue why or how she picked that venue, but there it was. More stories followed. Some made their way into the local paper and scholastic magazines and some her mom had bronzed.

In one capacity or another, Shelby has been writing all her life: advertising copy, political position papers, speeches, and mainstream fiction, but her greatest love of all is Erotic Romance. If there is anything more wonderful than exploring the eternal dance and love between those destined to find each other, she can't imagine it.

Her other favorite thing is hearing from readers. Readers should feel free to send Shelby an email at shelby.kentstewart@aol.com or leave a comment on her website at www.shelbykentstewart.com, where they can sign up for my Newsletter.

If you enjoyed this book, have a peek at her other books at Amazon.com/Shelby-Kent-Stewart/e/B00MD81ZEM/.

Coming Soon

FOR LOVE OF HONOR
Book 3 in the Wicked Tails Series

After running afoul of a nefarious criminal in her native Ireland, Pediatric Cardiologist Honor Delaney has faked her death and fled her homeland for the safety and obscurity of California's lush central coast.

Reinvented as Cassie Burrows, bartender extraordinaire, she lands a job at The Trident and catches the eye of Dr. Dylan Hunt, psychiatrist, armchair sleuth and royal pain in her ass.

Dylan didn't want to fall in love with the sexy vanilla bartender. He wanted a quick down-and-dirty encounter and then move on to greener pastures. But fate stepped in, and before he knew it, she was in his bed, his heart and they were both up to their necks in the kind of international intrigue that neither bargained for but must survive if they want a shot at happily ever after.

Author's Note

Domestic violence in the U.S. has reached epidemic proportions with close to one-third of American women reporting physical or sexual abuse by a husband or boyfriend at some point in their lives. In households with children where domestic violence occurs, the children are abused 60% of the time.

There are ways we can help. If you know someone at risk, find a way to let her know help is out there or report the abuse. Since most women suffering at the hands of a violent spouse or partner arrive at shelters and safe houses with nothing more than their children in tow and the clothes on their backs, donations of money and clothing are gratefully accepted. We're in this together.

U.S. Hotline: 800-799-SAFE (7233)
Teen Dating Abuse Hotline: 866-331-9474

Peace,

Shelby